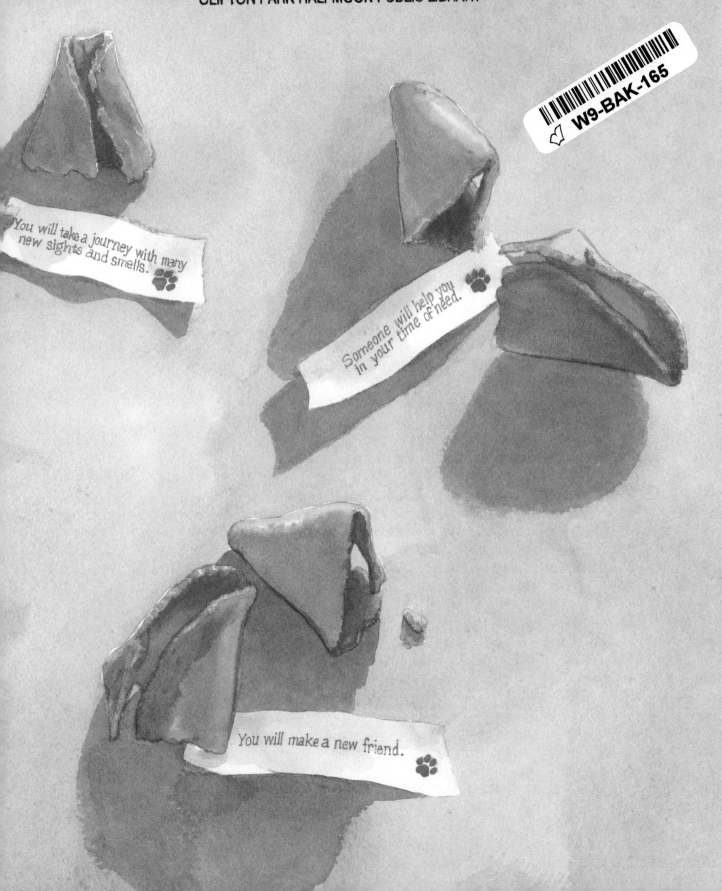

You will take a journey with many new sights and smells.

Someone will help you in your time of need.

You will make a new friend.

The Gryphon Press
—a voice for the voiceless—

These books are dedicated to those who foster compassion toward all animals.

For Metro, the Brooklyn rescue who inspired Cookie, and for all those animals still searching for a home.
—Lynda Graham-Barber

For Darcy, savior to hundreds of big (and small) dogs who needed good homes.
—Nancy Lane

Copyright © 2017 text by Lynda Graham-Barber
Copyright © 2017 art by Nancy Lane

Text set in Plantagenet Cherokee by Connie Kuhnz at Bookmobile Design and Digital Publisher Services
Printed in Canada

Library of Congress Cataloging-in-Publication Data
CIP data is on file with the Library of Congress.

ISBN: 9780940719392

1 3 5 7 9 10 8 6 4 2

I am the voice of the voiceless:
Through me, the dumb shall speak;
Till the deaf world's ear be made to hear
The cry of the wordless weak.

—from a poem by Ella Wheeler Wilcox, early 20th-century poet

COOKIE'S FORTUNE

Written by Lynda Graham-Barber   Illustrated by Nancy Lane

The little dog ran
and ran
and ran.
She ran until her tongue scraped the ground.

The little dog walked
and walked
and walked.
She walked until her paws
were raw and sore.

The little lost dog sniffed
and sniffed
and sniffed.
But nothing smelled like home.

It grew dark.
The little lost dog wandered into a junkyard,
weaving through row
after row
after row of rusted wrecks.

Weary, she climbed into a car
and fell asleep.
The car looked forgotten,
as forgotten as the little lost dog.

In the morning, she woke up hungry.
Sniffing the air, the little dog squeezed
through a hole in the metal fence.

Prickly burrs stuck to her fur.
The smells led the dog
to a big green dumpster.

She ripped open the bags and wrappers
scattered on the ground.

The hungry dog ate
and ate
and ate.
But the scraps did not taste like home.

One day, near the dumpster, the back door opened.
"Even a mutt's got to drink."
She lapped up the fresh water.

That night, snowflakes fell on the oily ground.
The little dog woke up shivering,
then wrapped her tail tightly around herself.
The forgotten dog and the forgotten car
stood stark against the pale pink dawn.

The next day
and the next day
and the day after that,
the little dog followed the smells to the dumpster.

When a lean, white dog chased her,
she scrambled through the fence,
past the prickly burrs,
back to the rusted car.
Safe inside, she licked her sticky paws
and scratched her matted fur.

Soon, the door by the dumpster opened again.
"Even a mutt's got to eat."
The little dog gobbled up all the food.

"Want a cookie?"
Cookie!
The dog sat up on her hind legs and begged
just as she remembered.

Leash in hand, the kneeling man spoke quietly. "It's okay."

Slowly the little brown dog followed the trail of food
and the encouraging words, "Good girl. G-o-o-d girl."

She nibbled at the treats, moving toward the kind voice,
a voice that reminded her of home.

The van pulled up to
the Last Chance Animal Shelter.
Inside, dogs barked
and whined
and howled.

The smells of forgotten
were everywhere.
A metal door rattled shut.
The tired dog curled up and slept.

People came to the shelter, day
after day
after day.
Some kennel doors opened.
A few dogs left.
Soon, more came to take their place.

But no one came for the little brown shelter dog.
Soon, she stopped dreaming of home.

One day, she awoke to the shuffle
of footsteps. The latch clicked.
Her door opened.

"What happened to her hair?"
asked a soft voice.

"We cut her hair short to get rid of all
the burrs and bubble gum," said the
volunteer.

"And we gave her three baths. She
smelled like soy sauce."

"What's her name?"

"We found her behind the Fortune Cookie restaurant,
so we call her Cookie."

Cookie!

Her eyes brightening,
the little dog sat up on her back legs
and raised her front paws,
high,
higher,
higher,
the highest she could raise them.

Her throat quivered with excitement.

Quiet hands
stroked her.

"Come on, Cookie.
Let's go home."

For Parents and Other Adults—Helping Dogs Like Cookie

Dogs are not our whole life, but they make our lives whole.
—ROGER A. CARAS, WRITER AND PHOTOGRAPHER

Cookie's story is all too common: a lost or abandoned dog ends up in a shelter. Cookie was lucky. By being adopted, she received that critical second chance. Dogs have become an indisputable part of our lives. There are 78.2 million dogs across the United States—that's one dog for every four Americans. Not only do they enrich us with their love and support, but dogs also act as service animals and detect dangerous devices and substances.

Yet every year, shelters in this country take in far more dogs than they adopt out. Five in ten dogs are euthanized because there are not enough safe homes in which to place them. This translates into about 8,200 dogs every day. Only 20 percent of companion dogs were adopted from shelters. Many were purchased from pet shops, and some of these dogs were born in breeding mills under unhealthy conditions. As if that weren't bad enough, every time an animal is purchased from a pet store, a dog in a shelter—like Cookie!—loses his or her chance to find a loving home

If you can't adopt a dog from a shelter now, you can still help homeless animals.

• ENCOURAGE FRIENDS AND FAMILY MEMBERS to have their pets spayed or neutered. A controlled population of healthy companion animals benefits everyone.

• CONTACT SHELTERS NEAR YOU to find out what volunteer help or supplies they need, because the needs vary by shelter.

• HOLD A BAKE OR RUMMAGE SALE to raise funds for a neighborhood shelter or animal-rescue group.

• ASK GROCERY AND FARM STORES TO DONATE bags of pet food (those damaged during shipping or with approaching expiration dates) to a shelter near you.

• CHECK WITH LOCAL GOVERNMENT REPRE-SENTATIVES about whether your state has laws that protect animals born in breeding facilities. Crowded, unsanitary cages result in sick puppies being sold in pet shops.

• CONSULT WEBSITES of animal rescue organizations for more information on what you can do to give a shelter animal a second chance, just as Cookie received in the story.

Tough cookies
never stop dreaming.

You will discover a
secret hideaway.